The Gr[eat] Classic Critters

Woodland Adventures for *Four Against Darkness*,
for characters of levels 4+

Written by Erick N. Bouchard

Illustrations by Andrea Sfiligoi

Additional materials: Andrea Sfiligoi, Jason Kemp.

Playtesters: Jason Kemp, Michael Lawing,
Scott Lewis, Pablo Miron.

For more info on the setting, visit:
https://sites.google.com/site/norindaal/

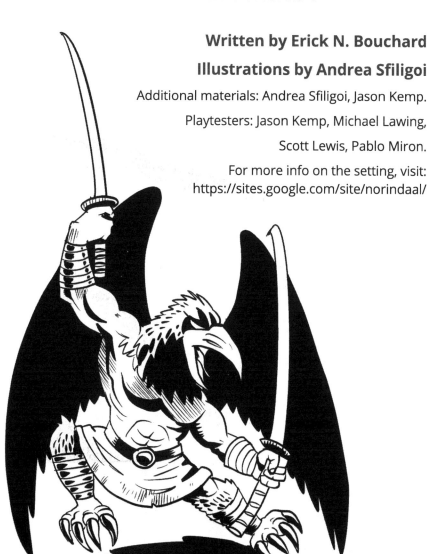

www.ganeshagames.net

Contents

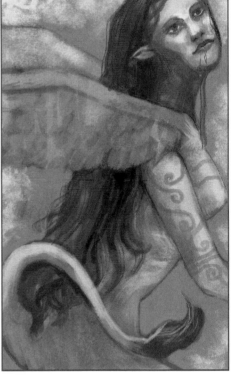

New Challenges!

As your characters gain levels, you will want new challenges to face and new monsters to fight. The *Crucible of Classic Critters* has been written to fulfill these cathartic urges to mercilessly kill imaginary creatures while adventuring in forest dungeons. It presents you with new tables for monsters, treasures and magic items to replace those in *Four Against Darkness* and new universal rules such as flying monsters and subduing.

To use this book, you only need the *Four Against Darkness* core rulebook.

Thematic Dungeons

This supplement offers tables for woodlands vermin, minions, Bosses, Weird Monsters and treasure.

Woodland dungeons are generated using the new area shapes from this book, which replace the room shapes in *Four Against Darkness*. Roll for room contents on the tables provided in this book. Traps, treasure, special events, spells found on scrolls and magic items change with the dungeon theme. The mechanics of the game (wandering monsters, using character abilities, combat, spell casting, clues, etc.) remain the same, unless the book says otherwise. You may use any secret, scroll or magic item in any books from the *Four Against Darkness* line, unless otherwise mentioned.

How to Use This Book

Upon starting a new dungeon, if all your characters are L4 or more, use the new tables herein instead of those from *Four Against Darkness*. The Quest table, the Epic Rewards table and the Hidden Treasure Complication table from the core book are still used.

Rolling for Areas

Use a map 20x28 squares in size for your woodlands dungeon. Roll d6+60 on the Woodlands Path Tiles table for the first tile and then d66 for all subsequent tiles. Consider "rooms" to be clearings and "corridors" to be paths. Rotate and mirror tiles as you see fit.

Area Content

To determine an area's content, roll on the Woodlands Area Content table instead of the Room Content table. The content of the squares in a given area, such as water or trees, may have special rules.

1

If a clear path to another tile is not available, you will have to swim or cut down trees to pass.

Feel free to mix the tables in this book with those of other books for variety and fun.

Acronyms

Only the *Four Against Darkness* core book (4AD) is required to play this book. Options are provided to create synergies with other books. The following acronyms refer to other books: *Dark Waters* (DW), *Knight of Destiny* (KoD), *Treasure Hunters of Charlemagne* (THOC), *Four Against the Abyss* (4AA), *Caverns of Chaos* (CoC), *Four Against the Netherworld* (4ATN), *The Courtship of the Flower Demons* (TCOTFD), *Seven Sisters* (SS), *Digressions of the Devouring Dead* (DDD), Greedy Gifts of the Guildmasters (GGG), *Revenge of the Ravenous Ratmen* (RRR), *More Monstrous Mayhem* (MMM), *Treacheries of the Troublesome Towns* (TTT), Fortress of the Warlord (FoTW).

Acknowledgements

Erick N. Bouchard © 2018. The author thanks Andrea Sfiligoi, Dave Arneson, Gary Gygax, Steve Jackson, Ian Livingstone, Don Turnbull, Jack Vance, James E. Raggi, Red Hook, the playtesters and all those who contribute to the Old School Renaissance movement for inspiration.

Woodlands Dungeons

The monsters featured in this book, while perfectly respectable dungeon denizens, are better suited for forested areas. The new area tables allow for a refreshing change of environment from the depressing gray of underground tunnels. Draw these "woodlands dungeons" as you would normally but draw trees or hatched lines instead of walls. The dense forest is impassable unless cut down.

Woodlands play out as regular dungeons except as follows:

Entrance Room: Roll d6+60 Woodlands Area Type table for your first tile. Do not roll for content. This area is empty and may be Searched if you want.

Rooms: Roll d66 with the Woodlands Area Type table for the other 15 tiles.

Doors: There are no doors and no locks to pick in woodlands.

Fire: Trees are highly flammable. Casting a fireball or another fire-based spell in a wood has a 1-2 in 6 chance of causing the area to be set aflame. From then on, passing through this area requires a L5 dragon breath save. Characters lose 2 life on a failed save, 1 life on a successful save. In addition, roll a d6 each time you return to this location: on a roll of 1, an adjacent woodlands area is also set aflame. The flames persist until the party exits the woodlands dungeon. You can extinguish flames with the Alter Weather and Water Jet spells.

Flyers: If the entire party is flying (e.g., riding flying mounts), they can fly over water and bridges. Any woodlands area becomes accessible. However, the party will be attacked normally by monsters when entering a woodlands area as they force it to land by hurling arrows, rocks, trees or the like. (See Flying Monsters below).

Woodlands Features

Some woodlands areas have unique features, as shown in the Woodlands Area Content table. Special rules apply when entering these areas.

Bridge: Roll a d6 for its type: 1-2 stone, 3-6 wood. If you want, you can use the rules for fighting in corridors when a bridge is present (4AD). Unless fighting aquatic or flying monsters, your party can retreat from a combat without suffering monster attacks in return by destroying the bridge. Wooden bridges can be destroyed with a Fireball or Lightning spell. If the bridge is adjacent to trees (e.g. tiles 25 and 42), the area may be set aflame (as per the rules described above). Stone bridges cannot be destroyed by Basic/Expert level characters (L1-9) unless using a bomb or a djinn's wish.

Trees: You don't have to draw individual trees. Simply use a green pen, draw circles or a similar symbol to save time if you prefer.

Your party can cut down 1 tree square in 20 minutes, allowing the party to move into the area (roll twice for wandering monsters, on a d6 roll of 1). This way, the party can move between two tiles blocked by a tree square. If at least 1 character is wielding an axe, it takes only 10 minutes (roll only once for wandering monsters).

Casting the Bountiful Harvest spell (TCOTFD) allows the party to lay a permanent path to cross a number of forest squares equal to the spellcasting roll or less (e.g. up to 6 tree squares with a spellcasting roll of 6).

Water: Crossing running water is possible by flying or swimming. Barbarians, swashbucklers, moonbeasts, icthyans, rangers and water-related classes can swim across water automatically. All other classes need to make a L3 swimming save for each square crossed or lose 1 life. Apply a -1 penalty for shield carriers and an additional penalty of -1 for light armor and -2 for heavy armor (not counting bikini armor). This penalty applies also to horses wearing barding. Halflings, dwarves and elves (other than sea elves, river elves and sea dwarves) are poor at swimming and suffer an additional -1 penalty.

Learning to swim counts as an Expert skill for all other classes (1 XP roll).

Characters who can breathe underwater always succeed at swimming saves.

Well: One or more party members can drink from a well or ignore it. Decide before rolling. Each character, retainer or mount can only drink from a well once. Roll a d6: 1 poisoned (make a L3 poison save or lose d3 life), 2-3 no effect, 4-6 heal 1 life.

Open–Sky Dungeons

If, for some reason, you want to encounter only flying monsters (e.g. your party is traveling in the open skies or on a magic cloud castle) roll d3 instead of d6 on any of the woodlands monster tables.

New Rules

The following rules apply to woodland dungeons. Some of them are simplified rules previously featured in other 4AD books.

Adjusting to Higher and Lower Levels

This supplement is designed for L4 characters. If the highest character level in your party is higher, add 1 to the number of vermin and minions, and +1 to L and life of Bosses and Weird Monsters, for every level above 4. For Expert parties (levels 6-9), also add 2 to the L of any saves. For parties under L4, do the reverse (minimum 1).

Characterization

Some encounters or items in this book require to specify a character's sex and virginal or marital status (e.g. unicorns react more gently towards virgin women). You can decide these details on the spot (note them on your characters' sheet) or before the game. You can even determine them randomly, as you prefer.

Food Rations

One day's rations in dried foodstuffs sell for 1 gp each. They can be used to bribe some wild animals and non-intelligent monsters. A character can carry up to 10 food rations at a time.

Flying Monsters

Flying monsters are attacked at +1 by ranged weapons. If the encounter happens in a large area or room (12 squares or more), the monsters fly and can only be hit by ranged weapons, spells, spears or polearms. In that case, ranged weapons can be used for the entire combat, not only the first turn.

Gaining Experience

XP rules remain the same as in *Four Against Darkness*, but vermin are more deadly. Add the number of vermin encounters from this book to minion encounters, and make an XP roll once the total of both is 10. Remember that you are counting the number of **encounters**, not the number of vermin met.

XP rolls for defeating monsters from this book are made at +1.

Leaders

You may encounter minions with a leader in a clearing as the result of a 12 on the Woodlands Area Contents table.

Choose one of your characters as your champion. The champion will be locked in mortal combat with the leader, while the rest of the party will fight the minions. Once all minions are dead, everyone may attack the leader, and vice versa. Minions with a leader will not make a morale roll until their leader is killed or flees.

If you have 4AA, use the complete rules for leaders found in that book instead.

Madness

Madness stands for a character's gradual descent into insanity. Those with 1 or more Madness refuse to share equipment or gold. When

Madness rises above a character's level, that character becomes insane and flees to a horrid, unknown fate (remove the character from play). Monsters never gain Madness.

Characters under L6 can choose to lose 2 life points instead of gaining 1 Madness point.

See 4AA for detailed rules on Madness and recovering sanity.

New Reaction: Capture

The monsters use non-lethal attacks to capture instead of killing the characters. Any character brought to zero life and left behind will be captured, bound and brought to a secret hideout. One monster (only) flees with the captive, but the other characters don't get to hit it as it flees. The remaining monsters keep fighting with the intent of capturing the party.

To find the hideout, you must spend 3 clues (either in this dungeon or any another location of your choice) on the "Someone has been imprisoned" secret from 4AD. The secret lair will be an underground cave (2d6 x 2d6 squares in size) adjacent to the location in which you spent the clues. The captives will be guarded by the same monsters: roll for their numbers as indicated in the table entry but double the result (e.g. 2d6 x 2 centaurs or 2 eyeball monsters).

Captive characters will be left with d3 life, stripped and all their equipment sold. There will be 3d6 more captives

(L0, 1 life) at any time, in addition to any captive characters. One of them will be unique and colorful; roll once on the Prisoner table in the appendix.

The captive character's companions can fight the monsters to recover their friend. If the monsters have a "bribe" or a non-violent reaction, the party can also attempt to buy them back (or woo them with a satyr, if applicable).

Roll 2d6 on the Slave Pen table (in the appendix) for each captured character when the group finds the secret hideout, adding the captive character's level to the roll.

Soul Cubes

Dark hags and demons trade not in gold but in soul cubes, made from the souls of the dead burned in magic furnaces. A single soul cube can restore one charge to any magic item. They are worth 50 gp or 50 necros (𝑵), in the currency of the Netherworld.

See *Four Against the Netherworld* for detailed rules about soul cubes.

Subduing Monsters

Some Weird Monsters and Bosses can be subdued (e.g., unicorns and griffins), and taken as mounts once tamed. To subdue a monster, your party must have a rope or chain and must either use the Sleep spell or fight with -1 on all Attack rolls (striking with the flat of the blade or trying to knock it out instead of killing it). The creatures

Forest goblin scouts rest on the banks of the Mikandar river.

recover ½ of their life (round down) within 10 minutes.

Except for beastmasters, a character can control a single subdued major monster (boss or weird monster). The rest must be abandoned. Subdued monsters can be ridden, sold for gladiator fights in large cities, or sold to wizards and alchemists (for organs). Selling monsters yields 5 gp per monster level.

Wooing & Milking Critters

Some supplements offer new rules that "unlock" new options with monsters:

Satyrs (TCOTFD): The following creatures (if female) can be wooed by a satyr: angels, centauresses, dark hags, djinns, harpies, imps, lamiae, owlfolk, sphinxes and stone giantesses.

Monster Milking (GGG): The following creatures (if female) can be milked once by a hero with the Monster Milking skill as long as their reaction is non-violent (e.g. peaceful, bribe, etc.): angels, centauresses, dark hags, djinns, griffins, harpies, imps, lamiae, milk elementals, mist rats, owlfolk, sphinxes, stone giantesses, unicorns.

Alchemical Ingredients

Alchemists are always looking for rare ingredients used in potion making. If you have TCOTFD, you can craft potions from the creatures in this book by harvesting the uncommon ingredients described below.

Otherwise, a bundle of ingredients can be sold for 5d6 gp.

In order to simplify accounting, ingredients are counted in bundles, not individual components. An encounter with a group of minions or vermin (whatever their number), or a single Boss or Weird Monster, provides only one bundle of ingredients. In narrative terms, component quality is more important than numbers.

Harvestable Ingredients

Angels: Their dying tears count as Shokoti's tongue. Used for restoring lost levels.

Capricorns: A bundle of horns count as garrulous foetors' spine dust. Used for potions of climbing.

Centaurs: A bundle of bladders count as flayed fay skin. Used for mind control, memory and truth potions.

Dark Hags: Their hair is used to brew the Balm of Nicodemus (see the Classic Critters Magic Items table).

Evil Squirrels: Wizards, alchemists and conservationists can use their tendons and spend 1 soul cube to craft a girdle of sex change (see the Woodlands Magic Items table).

Eyeball Monsters: Their brain counts as a kraken's eye. Used for poisons and hypnosis.

Harpies: A bundle of feathers counts as shark teeth. Used to resist fear.

Imps: A bundle of tails count as electric eel organs. Used for protection against time feeding monsters.

Lamias: A set of eyes counts as grave shifter's knuckles. Used for snake sedatives or flight potions.

Rakshasa: Their cerebellum counts as a boulder beast's liver. Used for controlling plants and curing chaos taint.

Stone Giants: Their toes are used for strength and flight potions.

Sphinxes: Their tongue counts as elven ghouls' marrow. Used for rejuvenation.

Unicorns: A single unicorn's horn counts as a bundle of stirges' proboscis, used to resist poison, or a bundle of black pearls. Horns are also used to brew the Balm of Nicodemus (see below).

The Balm of Nicodemus

Any wizard, alchemist or conservationist who mixes hag's hair with a unicorn horn can brew a Balm of Nicodemus before an adventure by rolling a L5 alchemy save (only alchemists add +L). The ingredients are spent, whether the roll succeeds or not.

Thrown at an undead monster as an attack action, the balm cancels the monster's immunity to non-magical weapons. If thrown by a wizard or an alchemist, it works automatically. If thrown by any other character, it has only a 2 in 6 chance of working.

The balm sells for 40 gp.

Aya the alchemist prepares the Balm of Nicodemus.

Domesticated Animals

The following animal companions and mounts can be bought as special retainers by characters of any level. An animal companion cannot be of higher level than its master.

No party member, except for a beastmaster, can have more than 1 fighting animal companion in addition to a mount. Purely decorative animals that do not partake into combat or game effects (e.g. mice, parrots) don't count. Animals cannot open or bash doors, read scrolls or interact with room content except through combat. They never incur Madness checks. Only mounts can carry equipment. Use common sense!

While animal companions are more fragile than characters, as they generally have fewer life points, beastmasters can upgrade them with their training bonus. While they can be given to a new master, animal companions can only benefit from a single beastmaster's bonuses at any time.

Except for warhounds, you don't have to make your pets participate in combat if you don't want to.

Lesser Necromancy (4AA) works normally on animals. Atrocities (from DDD) cannot have animal companions.

See MMM and FoTW for more animal companions and mounts.

Animal Companions

Hawks: Level 1, life 1, Attack -1, Defense +2. Hawks give the party +1 to orientation saves (see 4ATN and FoTW). A party with one or more hawks reduces by 1 in 6 the chance of being surprised by monsters, but only outdoors. This bonus stacks with those of warhounds. They can't attack in corridors. Cost: 20 gp.

Owls: Level 1, life 1, Attack -1, Defense +2. Owls can either attack in combat (at -1) or give their master +1 to their spellcasting rolls. Owls kill d6 rats or rat-like monsters (vermin only), which they hate, instead of their normal attack. They can't attack in corridors. Cost: 20 gp.

Peacocks: Level 0, life 1, Attack -2, Defense +0, morale -2. Peacocks give their owner a +1 bonus at wooing and seduction saves. They can't attack in corridors. Cost: 10 gp.

Warhounds: Level 1, life 2, Attack +1, Defense +0, morale +1. Dogs are loyal to a specific master: each time their master receives a wound, they will take the wound instead on themselves on a d6 roll of 5-6 (the master has no choice in this). A party with one or more warhounds reduces by 1 in 6 the chance of being surprised by monsters. This bonus stacks with those of hawks. Warhounds always stand beside their master in marching order. An armorer can craft custom-made light armor for a dog (+1 Defense) for 50 gold. Only warhounds and wolves can wear it. Cost: 20 gp.

Wildcats: Level 1, life 2, Attack +0, Defense +1, morale +0. Wildcats automatically kill d6 rats or rat-like monsters (vermin only), which they hate, instead of their normal attack. Against other foes, wildcats will capriciously refuse to partake in any combat on a d6 roll of 1. Cost: 20 gp.

Create Your Own

Feel free to modify the animal's type and looks when picking one of the examples above (e.g. a hawk's profile can stand for a falcon, a vampire bat or a very aggressive parrot, while a warhound is like a wolf in all but name.)

You can create your own animal companions by using common sense and the following guidelines: pick an appropriate (e.g. animal or animal-like) vermin monster from any 4AD book and lower its L by 2. Distribute its L between Attack and Defense bonuses as fits the animal's style (aggressive ones like boars have higher Attack, fast and flying ones have higher Defense). An animal's default price is 10 gp plus 10 x L and 10 per special ability.

Animal companions should not have exceptionally powerful abilities, such as a garrulous foetor's infinite spawning power (use your judgement), otherwise you'll spoil your own game.

Mounts

Outdoors (e.g. outside dungeons), each subdued mount can carry a single rider, moving at twice the usual travel rate when riding on land and thrice when flying (3 hexes per day instead of 1; see 4ATN and TNBTW). The character riding a mount at the front gets a +1 Attack bonus outdoors. Other riders can only attack with ranged weapons or spells.

A character of L5 or higher can spend 1 successful XP check to turn a subdued mount into a companion. The mount fights with an Attack and Defense bonus equal to ½ its L (round down), with maximum 1 attack. Each mount can carry 2 riders, or twice as much as a character, but not both at the same time. It can only carry this much when not flying. A flying mount can only fly when it carries no more than one rider, or the same weight that a character can carry. Two halflings (or creatures of similar size) count as a single rider. Ogre-sized characters can't ride flying mounts unless they are dragon-sized. Unicorns can only be ridden by virgin women. Mounts will not enter dungeons. Undead mounts can enter the Netherworld normally (eg. using Lesser Necromancy from 4AA or the Children of the Damned spell from DDD).

Boars: Level 3, morale +1, 1 attack, Attack +2, Defense +1. Boars are hard to kill: when life goes down to 0, the boar attacks for 1 last turn on a d6 roll of 3-6, then it dies. Only a single dwarf

or halfling-sized character can ride them. Cost: 40 gp.

Mules, Llamas & Zebras: Level 0, life 2, no attacks, Defense +0, morale -2. Each can carry 3 times as much as a character, but only a single rider. They are stubborn: they will refuse to cross a bridge or cross dangerous terrain on a d6 roll of 1. They cannot be used for mounted combat. Cost: 5 gp.

Riding Horses: Level 0, life 3, no attacks, Defense +0, morale -2. They cannot be used for mounted combat nor take hits meant for their riders. Cost: 10 gp.

Tigers & Giant Cats: Level 7, 5 life, 1 attack (when ridden), Attack +4, Defense +3, morale +0. Giant felines are unreliable and capricious; if their rider dies or becomes unconscious or paralyzed, they will attack the party as a L7 monster on a d6 roll of 1-2. Only barbarians and beastmasters can ride them. The monster must first be subdued by the character himself, alone. 1 XP must be spent to keep the monster as a mount once the adventure is over. Tiger riders travel outdoors at a horse's speed. Cost: N/A.

Warhorses: Level 2, life 3, 1 attack, Attack +1, Defense +1, morale +0. They CAN be used for mounted combat outdoors (e.g. in woodlands) and provide a +1 Attack bonus to the rider in the first position of the marching order. Cost: 10 gp. An armorer can craft light or heavy armor for a horse (barding) at 10 times the normal cost. Cost: 30 gp.

New Classes

Beastmaster

Masters of hunting and beasts, beastmasters specialize in teaching tricks to their animal companions, with which they form tight bonds. While any class can make use of a trained warhound or falcon, no one knows how to push an animal to fight in perfect coordination with its master like beastmasters do.

Abilities: Beastmasters add +½L (round down) to their own Attack rolls. Beastmasters also add +½L (round down) as a training bonus to their animal companion's Attack, Defense, save rolls and life points. This does not include mounts.

A beastmaster can have up to 1 animal companion for every 3 levels (round up): 1 at levels 1-3, 2 at levels 4-6, 3 at levels 7-9 and so on. You may split the beastmaster's training bonus among them as desired. Beastmasters cannot have animal companions whose monster L is above their own L.

Beastmasters can forfeit 1 successful XP check to give the level increase to a single animal companion instead. The level increases the animal's life by 1 and either its Attack or its Defense by +1. Its L cannot rise above its master's.

When beastmasters die or becomes unconscious or paralyzed, their animal companions lose their training bonus

but remain with the group (unless this goes against the limit of 1 animal companion per character). This can cause an animal to leave the party (e.g. death from shock at the master's death or leaving the party to mourn over their master's corpse). Animals companions without a beastmaster keep any levels gained. A new beastmaster of sufficiently high level can claim the lonely animal for his own and apply the training bonus.

Saves: Like barbarians. They have the same bonuses and penalties to saves.

Armor allowed: Light armor and shields.

Weapons allowed: All except firearms.

Starting equipment: Light armor, shield, hand weapon, animal companion (L0 or 1).

The Beastmaster may trade the shield and hand weapon for a two-handed weapon or a bow.

Starting wealth: 2d6 gp.

Expert skills available: Arcane Tanner, Brawler, Acute Hearing, Combat Acrobatics*, Commanding Presence, Danger Sense, Double Attack, Knife Throwing, Quick Footed, Sworn Enemy*, Vampire Hunter*, Whirlwind of Steel.

Life: 4 +L. A L1 beastmaster has 5 life.

Also applies to any animal that receives a training bonus of at least +1.

Example: A L3 beastmaster has a L1 warhound animal companion. With her +1 training bonus, the warhound's profile goes as follows: level 1, 3 life, 1 Attack at +2, Defense +1, saves +1, morale +2, takes the master's wounds on a d6 roll of 5-6, reduces by 1/6 the chance of monster surprise. At L4, her training bonus rises to +2 and she can take a second animal companion. She can either spread her training bonus among her two animals (+1 each) or give a +2 bonus to just one of them.

New Clerics

In addition to the gods in other books, you can devote your clerics to the deities below. Clerics devoted to a specific deity can use the Blessing power as described in 4AD or, at any time, can spend a Blessing to use the alternative powers described below.

Cleric of Elidra

Goddess of harmony and beauty, inventor of music, protector of the Eliphar (elf) race, direct emanation of the Cosmos and its harmony, it is Elidra who chose for the world the name Norindaal, which in Godspeech means "song". Elidra appears like a dignified elven dancer of incredible beauty and agility, clothed in silk ribbons.

Because Elidra's protected people (elves) came to Norindaal only at the end of the Century of Fire and Rain, the other gods sometimes call her the Latecomer. According to legend, the elves were sent to Norindaal in "Traveling Stones" - meteoritic wombs that protected them and kept them in suspended animation until the dwarves freed them. The dwarves still grumble about this being their worst mistake to this day. Elidra is aligned with Life and Peace.

At any time, clerics of Elidra can spend 1 Blessing to cast the Song of Charm spell instead. The cleric makes a music save vs. the monsters' L, adding +L. If successful, you may pick the monsters' reaction from those available. Casting this spell requires to play a musical instrument. You must have at least one free hand to do so. When making any save, clerics of Elidra can choose to save as either elves or clerics.

Cleric of Korimnos

The Golden Stag with a Thousand Antlers, Korimnos appears as a gigantic stag with an impressive array of antlers or as a horned man. A god of masculine pride and fertility, Korimnos protects forests, fauns, stagmen, centaurs, and is worshipped by all herbivore beast-men. Korimnos is aligned with Life and Light.

In the An-mòr continent, there is a mostly human and elven cult of Korimnos in the Broken Spine, the mountains north of Dorantia. This druidic religion is at odds with the alchemist guilds from the Eternal City who raid the mountain in search of rare flowers and minerals.

Korimnos is often accompanied by Saali, a white doe that can turn into a swarm of deadly brown bees. This Norindaalan insect is similar to the Terran honeybee, but larger and with a potentially fatal sting. For this reason, beekeepers carry a deer motif on their clothes and protective equipment, and halflings bakers make doe-shaped honey biscuits.

At any time, clerics of Korimnos can spend 1 Blessing to make a natural animal or a group of them (e.g. any creatures that also exist in the real world) automatically have a peaceful reaction. Korimnos' clerics can woo as halflings and can craft potions as wizards.

In game terms, all clerics are humans. If you want an "elf cleric of Korimnos", just use this class and "pretend" she's an elf. Don't give her the elf class' abilities too!

Woodlands Area Content table (2d6)

2	**Treasure found:** Roll on the Woodlands Treasure table.
3	**Hunted:** Spend 1 clue or double the number of monsters in your next encounter with minions or vermin.
4	**Special Event:** Roll on the Woodlands Special Events table.
5	**Bountiful Game:** Each character heals 1 life.*
6	**Vermin:** Roll on the Woodlands Vermin table.
7	**Minions:** Roll on the Woodlands Minions table.
8	**Minions:** If corridor (path), empty. Otherwise, roll on the Woodlands Minions table.
9	**Trail:** Get 1 clue.
10	**Weird Monster:** Roll on Woodlands Weird Monsters table.
11	**Boss:** Roll on the Woodlands Boss table.**
12	**War Party:** If a corridor (path), roll on the Woodlands Boss table. If a room, you encounter both a Boss and its retinue of minions. (See Leader under New Rules.)

If your group includes a wandering alchemist, you also find d3 Common Ingredients which can be sold for d6 gp each or used to craft potions (see TCOTDF).

** *Roll d6. Add +1 for every Boss or Weird Monster that you have encountered so far in the game. If your total is 6+, or if the dungeon layout is complete, this is the Final Boss.*

ANDREA
STILIGOI
2020

Woodlands Area Type table (d66)

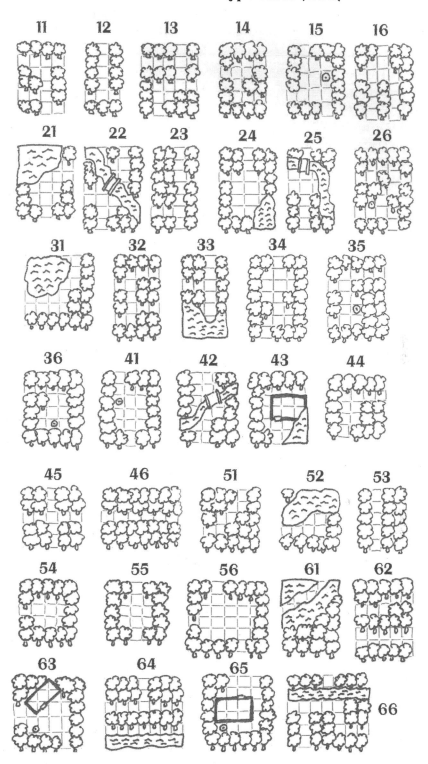

An axe is an invaluable tool when exploring woodland dungeons, as it can chop impassable vegetation and monsters' skulls in the same way.

Woodlands Vermin table (d6)*

1

2d6 Mist Rats. Level 3 flying vermin, no treasure, morale +1. Instead of attacking, a swarm of mist rats will gnaw at the party's foodstuffs and paper items. Each turn, a single mist rat will destroy (in that order) a piece of cheese, one day's food rations, a scroll, a leather object, any other non-metal object. They never harm xwarts or lantern bearers (carrying them is not enough; they must be held in hand).

Reaction: always gnaw at party's stuff.

2

d6+1 Imps. Level 5 flying hellspawn vermin, Woodlands treasure -1, morale -1. On a failed Defense roll, the character suffers no damage but loses a random object as a single imp flees away with it. A single vial of holy water thrown at them kills two imps. A Blessing spell cast by a cleric of god of Light causes d6+L imps to flee without stealing anything. Subtract 1 from their level per demonologist in the party. Imps never harm clerics of Akerbeltz but hate witchhunters.

Reactions (d6): 1-3 puzzle, 4-6 fight.

3

d6 Winged Capricorns. Level 4 flying vermin, no treasure, morale -1. On the first turn, the charging males fight like level 6 monsters (for both Attack and Defense). In addition to the males, the herd includes 2d6 non-combatant females and young (level 2 vermin, always flee). Winged capricorns are always met near a pond or river, which they fertilize: all characters regain 1 life the first time they drink from it.

Reactions (d6): 1-3 flee if outnumbered, 4-6 fight.

4

2d6 Carrion Worms. Level 4 vermin, Woodlands treasure -2. When hit by a carrion worm, a character must succeed a level 2 poison save or be paralyzed for the next turn. Moonbeasts and plague doctors are immune. Paralyzed characters cannot attack and fail all Defense rolls but can make poison saves normally.

Reactions (d6): 1-2 peaceful, 3-6 fight.

5

d6+3 Woodlands Wolves. Level 3 vermin, no treasure. Wolves fear fire and must check morale whenever 2 wolves are killed with a Fireball spell. If this attack drives their numbers below 50%, roll 2 morale checks. Subtract 1 from their morale rolls per beastmaster or ranger in your party (maximum -2).

Reactions (d6): 1 flee, 2-3 bribe (d3 food ration each), 4-6 fight.

6

2d6 Evil Squirrels. Level 3 rattish vermin, no treasure. Used as familiars by the witches of Mount Larrun, they steal their targets' luck and energy. On the squirrels' turn, instead of attacking, roll a d6 for all characters and add their level. If the roll is under the squirrels' current number, the character loses 1 luck point, 1 piety point, 1 panache point, 1 unspent spell/clerical power or 1 life (in that order). They never harm female wizards, clerics of Akerbeltz or Radah, mutants or necromancers. Evil squirrels hate paladins and witchhunters (see *note 8*).

Reaction: always fight.

---

* *If you get the same result on this table twice in a row and you have either of these books, you may either roll on THOC's Wild Animal table, lowering all monster levels by 2, or MMM's Crag Vermin table, for greater variety. If you have both books, choose or pick one at random.*

Rakshasas are demonic masters of illusion that can alter the flow of time with their sorcery. They look like bestial humanoids with long-fanged, tiger-like faces.

Woodlands Minions table (d6)*

1   **d6+1 Harpies.** Level 7 flying minions, Woodlands treasure. On each of the harpies' turns, all characters must succeed a L4 magic save or be paralyzed by their song for the entire round. Wizards, halflings, satyrs, clerics of Akerbeltz and bards add +½L. Deaf characters are immune. Paralyzed characters cannot attack and fail Defense rolls automatically. Harpies are immune to Sleep. Bards can pacify them with a L7 music save (add ½ their bard level).

*Reactions (d6): 1-2 quest (always "Bring me that!"**), 3-4 bribe (1 gem each), 5-6 fight.*

2   **d3+1 Owlfolk Riding Dogs.** Level 8 flying minions, Woodlands treasure -1, 2 attacks each. An owlman's and its mount's attacks always strike the same target. If both hit, they stop flying but automatically inflict 1 more wound on each of their turns. Fire spells cause them a -1 morale penalty. Subtract 1 from the reaction rolls for each owl or conservationist in the party.

Reactions (d6): 1-2 merchant (see note 9), 3-4 bribe (d6 food rations each), 5-6 fight.

3   **d6+2 Giant Eagles.** Level 7 flying minions, treasure: d6 gems worth d6 x 3 gp each. Giant eagles fight at -2 to their L in corridors. Except in corridors, if at least 3 attacks succeed against a single character, the character must succeed a L4 Defense roll or be swept away, never to be seen again. The characters have a single turn to kill the eagles carrying their companion with a ranged weapon or spell. Any attack roll of 1 hits their unfortunate companion instead, without any chance of a Defense roll.

Reactions (d6): 1 flee, 2 peaceful, 3-4 bribe (1 gem of any value each), 5-6 fight.

4   **d6 Living Wheels.** Level 5 chaos minions, Woodlands treasure -1. The rolling, disc-shaped mutants will surprise the party on a d6 roll of 1-3. If they surprise, they throw knives with their four hands before combat, forcing each character to make a L3 Defense roll or lose d3 life. Subtract 1 from their reactions per atrocity, mutant or chaos golem in the party.

Reactions (d6): 0 (or less) offer food and drink, 1-3 bribe (10 gp each), 4-6 fight.

5   **2d6 Centaurs.** Level 5 minions, Woodlands treasure -1. Their blood is poisonous: any successful melee attack forces the attacker to save vs. L2 poison or lose 1 life. Centaurs surprise on a d6 roll of 1-2. If the party includes any female members, their reaction is always "capture".

Reactions (d6): 1 offer food and rest, 2-3 merchant (sells any item under 101 gp from the 4AD core book), 4 capture, 5 bribe (2d6 gold each), 6 fight.

6   **d6+2 Troglodyte Lizardmen.** Level 7 minions, Woodlands treasure +1. Before combat, all party members must save vs. L3 poison save or retch uncontrollably, unable to stand the monsters' skunk-like smell. Retching characters cannot attack for the first d3 turns of combat. Alchemists, cheesemeisters and plague doctors are immune. If cast immediately before combat, a Protect spell will also make 1 party member immune to the smell. Fireball spells cause troglodytes to check morale. Lower their morale by 1 per atrocity in the party.

Reaction: Always fight.

---

* If you get the same result on this table twice in a row and you have either of these books, you can either roll d6 (not d8!) on THOC's Monster table (lower all monster levels by 2), KoD's Day Minions table (ignore any references to Piety, Hunters, relics and the Challenge table) or MMM's Crag Minions table, for greater variety. If you have both books, choose or pick one at random. For each encounter during which a Legendary Item from THOC is used, the user gains 1 Madness point.

** From then on, every time the party kills a Weird Monster or Boss, there is a 1 in 6 chance that it will have the object sought (a silver mirror) in addition to its treasure, if any. A sphinx will always have such a mirror if you have this quest and will surrender it if its puzzle is achieved. To complete the quest, the party must bring the object back to the harpies.

Woodlands Weird Monsters table (d6)

1 — **Angel of Light*.** Level 8 flying Weird Monster, 5 life, 2 attacks +1 attack per miscreant (see note 1), morale +2, treasure: Blessing scroll & Invocation of Order (if you have *Caverns of Chaos*, otherwise a jewel worth 30 gp). Angels of Light hate miscreants and cause them 2 wounds per hit. Spellcasting by miscreants is at -2. Immune to Sleep.

Reactions: See note 1.

2 — **Griffin*.** Level 6 flying Weird Monster, 4 life, 3 attacks, 2 Woodlands treasures +1. Sleep spells affect griffins at -1. Subtract 1 from its reactions per beastmaster or conservationist in the party.

Reactions (d6): 1 peaceful, 2-3 bribe (d6 food rations), 3-4 fight.

3 — **Sphinx*.** Level 7 flying Weird Monster, 6 life, 3 attacks, morale +1, 2 Woodlands treasures. Increase its L by 2 if the party attacks before solving the puzzle. Wizards, conservationists, rogues and gnomes add +L to the puzzle roll. Immune to Sleep.

Reaction: always puzzle.

4 — **Elemental.** Level 6 Weird Monster (hellspawn), life 6, normal Woodlands treasure, never check morale. Roll a d6 for the elemental's subtype: 1 earth (slashing weapons attack at -1), 2 air (flying monster; blunt weapons attack at -1), 3 fire (immune to fire-based spells and attacks), 4 water** (ranged weapons attack at -1), 5 lightning (flying, immune to lightning, non-gilded metal weapons attack at -1), 6 energy (save vs. L3 energy drain when hit or lose 1 level). All elementals are immune to Sleep. Gilded weapons attack them at +2. Demonologists can possess them (see 4ATN).

Reaction: always fight.

5 — **Lamia.** Level 7 Weird Monster, 6 life, 2 attacks, Woodlands treasure +3 and 1 soul cube. Any target losing life to the lamia must succeed a L3 magic save or lose 1 level until Blessed. At the end of each of your party's turns, roll 2d6. If the result is under the lamia's current life, your party had been fighting a double all along: restore her life to 6. Immune to Sleep. Subtract ½ the level of any female wizard or cleric of Akelbertz in the party from her reactions.

Reactions (d6): 1 quest (always "Slay all the monsters!"), 2-3 bribe (a jewel worth 100 gp or more), 4 magic challenge, 5-6 fight until a character dies then flee with the corpse.

6 — **Unicorn.** Level 6 Weird Monster, 6 life, 1 attack, no treasure, morale -1. Unicorns do d3 damage with their enchanted horn. If a 3 is rolled, make another attack against the same character (once). They are immune to Sleep and poison. Subdued unicorns can only be ridden by virgin women. Subtract 2 from the unicorns' reactions if the group includes one or more female virgins of any species or a unicorc (from MMM). A wizard can use 1 soul cube and 1 unicorn horn to turn the horn into a magic knife (slashing light weapon +1, for a net attack bonus of +0) who gives its user +2 on saves vs. poison. Unicorns hate cambions, atrocities, mutants, necromancers, succubi and clerics of the Death gods.

Reactions (d6): 1 peaceful, 2-4 flee, 5 bribe (any magic food), 6 fight.

* These monsters can be subdued. A sphinx whose riddle is solved is subdued. Subdued angels can carry your character instead of being ridden if the thought makes you uncomfortable. (It's far less funny though.) Angels can carry only one rider.

** If your party includes a cheesemeister (RRR), roll a d6 when encountering a water elemental: on a roll of 5-6, it is a milk elemental instead. Its reaction is always peaceful when a cheesemeister is present, and it can be milked. Cheese made from milk elementals works like holy water and also heal 1 life. It sells for 30 gp.

Woodlands Boss table (d6)*

1 **Eyeball Monster.** Level 8 flying Boss, 6 life, 2 attacks per party member, 2 Woodlands treasures+2, morale +2. Immune to Sleep. Spellcasting rolls are at -2. At the beginning of each of the monster's turns, all party members who succeed a L5 magic save (wizards and halflings add +½L) reduce the monster's number of attacks against them by 1. Ice elf huntresses succeed automatically. You can puncture the monster's main anti-magic eye with a successful Attack at -3: doing so inflicts no damage on the creature but it cancels spellcasting penalties and reduces its attacks to 1 per party member (the number of attacks cannot be reduced to fewer than 1 attack per party member)

Reactions (d6): 1 quest (always "Bring me that!"), 2 bribe (all the party's magic items), 3 magic challenge (at -2 for the challenging character), 4 capture, 5-6 fight.

2 **Djinn.** Level 6 flying Boss, 5 life, 1 attack (special), Woodlands treasure, morale -1. Immune to Sleep. In addition to his normal attacks, a djinn has 1 additional lightning attack against shield bearers and 1 more against characters wearing heavy armor or made of metal (e.g. golems). Djinns are cowards: they are always considered subdued when they would flee *(see note 3)*.

Reactions (d6): 1 quest (always "Bring me gold!"), 2 friendly, 3-4 magic challenge, 5-6 fight.

3 **Coatl (feathered dragon).** Level 6 flying Boss, 5 life, 3 attacks, Woodlands treasure. Immune to Sleep. Those bitten by a coatl must succeed a L3 poison save or fall comatose until the end of combat (those abandoned are eaten). Halflings, barbarians and dwarves add +½L to the save.

Reactions (d6): 1 quest, 2 flee, 3-6 fight.

4 **Dark Hag.** Level 7 demon Boss, 6 life, 2 attacks, never checks morale, 1 Woodlands Magic treasure, 1 random Basic level scroll (from any 4AD book you own) and d3 soul cubes. The hag dies instantly if a witchhunter's or a paladin's Attack rolls exactly 13. At the beginning of each of her turns, the hag will attempt to capture the character with the highest net Attack bonus inside her boiling cauldron (only one at a time). A successful L5 strength save is needed to escape. Warriors and paladins add +½L, moonbeasts, green trolls and ogre-sized characters add +L. Halflings save at -1. The character inside the cauldron cannot attack and loses 1 life each turn from the heat, unless immune to fire. The hag loses 1 Attack while she's got a captive in her cauldron (as she prevents her meal's escape). In addition to her Attacks, the hag will cast a spell *(see note 2)*. She hates witchhunters. The hag is immune to Sleep.

Reactions (d6): 1-2 quest (see note 2), 3-4 bribe (all magic items), 5-6 capture.

5 **Rakshasa.** Level 7 demon Boss, 6 life, 3 attacks, 3 Woodlands Magic treasures +1 magic item of your choice from the Magic Item table in 4AD. Rakshasas are masters of illusion and sorcery. Take notes or pictures of your characters' sheet before combat begins. On the rakshasa's turn, roll a d6. If the result is 1, the rakshasa reverses time and you must start to fight it again as if it was the first turn, resetting the life and other abilities of everyone as they were at the beginning of combat. Casting any Temporal spell (from MMM) cancels this ability instead of the spell's usual effect. The Rakshasa is immune to Sleep.

Reactions (d6): 1 quest (always "Bring me his head!"), 2-3 bribe (50 gp), 4-6 capture.

6 **Stone Giant.** Level 8 Boss, 6 life, 2 attacks, d3 damage per hit, morale +1, 2 Woodlands treasures. In dungeons (not outdoors), stone giants surprise parties on a d6 roll of 1-2. If hostile, they will shoot a rock at the party, causing the 2 characters in the front of the marching order to roll a successful L5 save (rogues add +½L) or be hit for d3 damage. Immune to Sleep.

Reactions (d6): 1-2 quest (always "Let peace be your way!"), 3-4 bribe (50 gp), 5 capture, 6 fight.

* If you get the same result on this table twice in a row and you have KoD, you may roll on its Side Quest table instead. Ignore any reference to hunters and dishonor, and replace any rumors gained with clues.

Woodlands Treasure table (d6)

0	Nothing*.
1	d6 x 4 gp or any single item worth 20 gp or less in the 4AD book**.
2	One gem worth 2d6 x 5 gp**.
3	Roll for a scroll on the Random Spell table from 4AD or 1 vial of holy water.
4	Roll on the Useless Spell Scroll table or 5d6 x2 gp.
5	One item of jewelry worth 4d6 x10 gp.
6+	Roll on the Woodlands Magic Treasure table.

If you have the Man-Eater! book, you may roll on the Forest of Thraa Unique Events table instead if you wish. Halflings can spend 1 Luck point to re-roll the result.

** *If your party includes a wandering alchemist, you can find instead either d6+1 random Common Ingredients or d3 Uncommon or Mineral Ingredients (TCOTFD). Alternately, the alchemist manages to brew any single potion of your choice worth 2d6 x5 gp or less.*

Useless Spell Scroll table (d6)*

1	**Delay Chores:** This powerful spell affects true reality (not just the game). When cast, show your spouse or parents the following lines: The present spell entitles you, the actual player (not your characters), to delay any chores or bedtime by exactly one hour so you can keep playing *Four Against Darkness*. It can only be cast once per day.
2	**Suicidal Pyre:** When this spell is cast, the caster burns his or her own soul to create a single soul cube. The soul cube can be used (by someone else) to give one charge to any magic item. The caster dies as soon as the last casting word is uttered and cannot be resurrected or raised as an undead by any means (as the soul is irreversibly destroyed). Retainers and captives will never cast this spell.
3	**Solipsist Genocide:** This mass destruction spell immediately kills 1,000 people times the caster's level. The targets are random living beings which the caster has never seen or heard from, nor ever see any sign they ever existed. Likewise, you will never know if the spell worked or not (make the spellcasting roll with your eyes closed.)
4	**Infuriate God:** This spell grievously insults an unknown god, who immediately takes retribution against the caster by causing his or her spectacular death. All onlookers gain 1 Madness. If cast in a town, all citizens become insane (leave quickly!)
5	**Cancel Dissipation:** When cast, this spell immediately cancels its own effect. It cannot be canceled, even by a wish.
6	**Universal Annihilation:** This spell, the most powerful to have ever existed, has never been cast yet. When cast, the entire universe of Norindaal is destroyed. You must immediately burn all your 4AD books to cinders, delete all files and stop playing. For the spell to be completely effective, you must buy all copies of the game you can find (including print-on-demand copies) and burn them too. For obvious reasons, every inhabitant of Norindaal will want the caster dead. Unfortunately, casting the spell takes a year of chanting (in game time), during which one of each monster in every 4AD book you own will attempt to kill your character, one after the other. You must play these combats one by one before the spell takes effect.

* These unusual spells can only be cast by wizards, conservationists or necromancers. Despite their complete and irrefutable uselessness, these scrolls still sell for 75 gp each. Carrying (not to mention casting) the Universal Annihilation spell is punishable by death in all towns of Norindaal.

Woodlands Magic Treasure table (d6)

1	**Girdle of Sex Change:** Designed as a curse against a king's heir, the item has attracted the attention of Gobras, god of jesters. Aside for the obvious effect, which wears off after d6 games, the belt allows the wearer to cast the Blessing spell once. It cannot be taken off until its effect wears off. Artificial beings cannot use it. (*See note 7*). Selling price: 2d6 gp.
2	**Talisman of Vigilance:** This eye-shaped pendant, worn in the back, reduces by 1 in 6 the chance of being surprised. It does not work if the talisman is not able to "see" from its position (e.g. in total darkness or with a shield upon the wearer's back) or if the foes are invisible. Selling price: 100 gp.
3	**Scarab of Undeath:** This disturbing, worm-like brooch forces the first character touching it when the treasure is found (roll randomly) to make a L6 magic save or die. Necromancers add +L to the save. If a companion pins the brooch on the dead character's chest, s/he will raise from the dead as a sentient undead. The raised character keeps all former abilities and can raise in levels normally, but can no longer eat, drink, procreate, sleep, breathe, suffers cold damage or benefit from potions. Except in cold or dry environments (e.g. the arctic, deserts or the Netherworld), rot will cause the character to smell horrible and decompose, causing the party to fail at any social type save (except vs. undead). For the purposes of spells, magic items or Expert skills (e.g. Turn Undead or Healing Surge), the character is considered a vampire, albeit a decomposing one. If the brooch is ever removed, the character dies and the Scarab loses all powers. The brooch has no effect on artificial and undead beings. Selling price: 66 gp.
4	**Bow of Speed:** This enchanted bow can fire an additional arrow (2 instead of 1) on the first turn of combat, including arrows of slaying (from the Epic Reward table in 4AD). If the user can already shoot more than 1 arrow per turn, the Bow of Speed adds 1 shooting attack. Selling price: 200 gp.
5	**Balm of Nicodemus:** Thrown at an undead monster as an attack action, this potion cancels its immunity to non-magical weapons. If thrown by a wizard or an alchemist, it works automatically. If thrown by any other character, it has only a 2 in 6 chance of working. Selling price: 40 gp.
6	**Cloak of Darkness:** When the hood of this cloak is pulled over the wearer's head, the wearer becomes invisible. Unfortunately, all sources of light in the room or location (including the party's lantern) immediately shut down in total darkness. Only the wearer can see clearly in darkness (but cannot read and use scrolls under these conditions), and benefits from a +3 Defense bonus. All other characters are blinded and suffer a -2 penalty to all rolls. Selling price: 100 gp.

28

Woodlands Special Events table (d6)*

1 **Forest Fire:** Fighting the fire is resolved as a combat against a L5 Weird Monster with 1 life (minimum 3) per adjacent tree square in the tile (pick the largest zone available). Never checks morale, immune to magic (except Quelch Fire from TTT, or the spells Water Jet and Alter Weather from W&A). Only shields protect against it. Fighting the fire involves cutting down trees. Characters with axes have +2 to Attack rolls. Each life point taken from the monster counts as cutting down 1 tree square (see Woodlands Features).

2 **Stampede:** An animal herd runs wildly across the woods. All characters must make a L3 running save or lose d3 life. On a roll of 1, they lose all hand-held items too. Barbarians and elves add +1, small characters (lutins, dwarves, goblins, halflings, etc.) roll at -1.

3 **Pegasi:** You encounter d3 flying horses, peacefully grazing. If you succeed a L5 taming save (one separate roll per pegasus), you can use them as mounts. Beastmasters add +L, barbarians add +½L, halflings add +1 and can use 1 Luck point to re-roll. Mounted fighters have +1 to Attack rolls outdoors. When travelling in the wilderness, flying mounts move at triple rate. A pegasus can carry 2 riders and their equipment. Two halfling-sized characters count as a single rider. If you roll this result again, see *note 6*.

4 **Wanton Frolic:** Your party comes upon satyrs and dryads engaging in energetic merriment. Make a L3 breeding save for every character who joins them (your choice), excluding monks, shrews and their spouses. Halflings and swashbucklers add +½ L, satyrs automatically succeed. Those who succeed gain 1 clue and heal d3 life, those who fail lose 1 life from exhaustion.

5 **Captive Found:** Get 1 clue and roll on the Prisoner table. Roll d6: on a 1-3, the prisoner is guarded by a hidden pit: L4 trap, subtract the armor bonus from the save, rogues add +L, halflings and elves add +1. Lose 1 life on a failure. A lone character who falls in the pit dies unless a L6 climb save is made. A single witchhunter can torture the captive for 1 clue as for witches.

6 **Treasure Map:** Get d3 clues. They can only be spent to find a hidden treasure (see 4AD). If your party has a spade, only 2 clues are needed for it.

* If you get the same result on this table twice in a row and you have the Three Rings book, you may roll d66 on that book's main table instead. Should you find Davanzu's rings, you can sell them back to him for 100 gp each if you meet him in the future. Alternately, to add even more variety, you may either roll on Man-Eater!'s Forest of Thraa Wandering Monsters table (add 2 to all monster levels) or roll on MMM's Special Events table. If you have all these books, pick one at random or choose.

Slave Pen table (2d6+captive character's L)	
Roll separately for each character	
2-9	Roll d6. On a 1-3, the prisoner was eaten and is lost forever. On a 4-6, the prisoner was killed. The corpse can be resurrected.
10-11	Character can be bought for the price of a bribe. If not is indicated, the bribe is 2d6 gp per character level. The bribe for 0-level characters is d6 gp.
12-14	The character was sold as a slave. You find the prisoner as part of the treasure of the next Boss monster you encounter.
15+	The character was sold as a slave. You find the prisoner as part of the treasure of the next Final Boss you encounter.

Prisoner table (d66)

11-14	**Pernicious Princess:** The infuriated aristocrat wants vengeance against all those who humiliated her. The party gets an Epic Reward if they complete the "Slay all the monsters!" quest for the present dungeon (4AD). She insists on walking in the first rank and to have at one character or retainer on the second row behind her carry her gown's train (which requires at least one hand), otherwise her persistent whining causes the party a -1 penalty to all ranged attacks and spellcasting. **
15-22	**Miserly Merchant:** His goods were stolen and he desperately wants them back. The party gets an Epic Reward for completing the "Bring me that!" quest (4AD), except that the quest object is the merchant's stash (cargo and hard-to-sell baubles) instead of a magic item.
23-26	**Helpful Healer:** Glad to be saved, the healer can restore 1 life point to each party member. If you have TCOTDF and fewer than 5 characters, she can join the party as a wandering alchemist of a level equal to the party's lowest level. If not, but you have BBB, she can join the party as a succubus of the same level. Otherwise, the healer will simply give the party a reward of d6 x 5 gp when returned home.
31-34	**Cheerful Cleric:** The enthusiastic priest gladly offers the party to cast them as single Blessing spell, now or at any later time of their choice. If the party engages in drinking alcohol or fornication in the cleric's presence, he will pester them with sermons for the rest of the dungeon until brought home (-1 to all spell casting, puzzle and will saves). *(See note 4.)*
35-42	**Sinister Spy:** She knows d3 clues and will give them to the party in exchange for being accompanied to safety. If the party is under 4 characters, she can join them as a rogue, a harlequin or an assassin of a level equal to the party's lowest level.
43-46	**Desperate Dwarf:** The miserly fellow buried his treasure not far from here but lost his bodyguards and needs to be escorted there. The party is given the "Bring me that!" quest (4AD). The magic item is an ancient dwarf heirloom (a magic tobacco pipe that heals 1 life after each combat, worth 250 gp). The quest's reward is always the Gold of Kerrak Dar (4AD) and is only offered when the dwarf is safely escorted out of the woodlands with his pipe in hand. There is a 1 in 6 chance that you encounter Harros Davanzu instead *(see note 5)*.
51-54	**Poor Peasant:** Once the adventure is over, the rescued peasant will offer the party d6+3 food rations (worth 1 gp each) as a thank you gesture. He will also happily offer his many daughters and sons in marriage to any interested character. **
55-62	**Inebriated Innkeeper:** Once returned to safety (outside the dungeon), the grateful innkeeper promises the party free alcoholic drinks at his establishment for the rest of their adventuring careers. If you wish, any or all characters may roll their first fear or Madness save when starting a new dungeon or adventure, but also suffer a -1 penalty to ranged attacks due to drunkenness.
63-66	**Thoughtful Teacher:** Once the adventure is over and he is safely returned home, the old fellow can teach a single character of Expert level an Expert skill for free (no XP needed). The trained character must miss the next adventure to do so. The skill must be available for the character's class. If the entire party is under L6, the teacher's offer remains available in the future when they level up.

Feel free to change any prisoner's gender or to randomize it. You may also roll on this table anytime you reveal the secret "Someone has been imprisoned" (4AD).

**If you have 4 or fewer characters, the prisoner can marry a character after the adventure and join the party as a 5th character (e.g. princess-in-distress from GGG or shrew from RRR) of their spouse's level. Otherwise, they are simply a L0 retainer with 2 life, no bonuses, morale -1 and proficiency only in light weapons. Polygamous characters only get a +1 bonus for additional shrews after the first but suffer the cumulative penalties.

Notes to Tables

Note 1 (Angel of Light): Angels are notoriously uncompromising servants of the gods of Light, Law and Life. The angel of Light will always fight to the death a party that includes at least one character of the following classes: demonologists, cambions, all classes from DDD except Clerics of Darim, moonbeasts, succubi, any character Touched by Chaos, bearing an Abominable Gift (from 4ATN) or any character devoted to a deity of the Demons, Chaos or Death alignments. All of these characters are thereafter labeled as "miscreants".

Otherwise, the angel of Light offers food and drink, and casts a Blessing on the party. Parties which do not include any miscreants and include at least 1 character devoted to a Light deity, with a rope or chain, can subdue the angel of Light. Angels can be used as mounts (or "carriers") only when flying, and will only carry one passenger.

A demonologist can also forcibly subdue an angel to serve him as a mount using the demonologist's possession power (see 4ATN). The will-broken angel will become the demonologist's slave, not fighting in combat but neither taking the place of a possessed creature. A

subdued angel can be sold for 100 necros to Salamandrine Men or in the Netherworld.

If you have TTT, you can roll on the Gods of Light table for the angel's patron deity.

Angels of Light are very rare. If you roll this encounter again, you encounter a **Sabertooth Tiger**: Level 7 Weird Monster, 5 life, 2 attacks, morale +0, no treasure. A barbarian who subdues the tiger in single-handed combat (with no help from the rest of the party) can ride it as a mount.

Other types of Angels, called Anserti or Ansari in the Trade Language of Norindaal, exist, and are devoted to serving other gods or other causes.

Note 2 (Dark Hag): Her quest is "I want him alive!". Roll d6 at the end of each of the hag's turns, adding +1 if she is under ½ her original life, and apply the results that follow:

1-2 Giant Frog Monster: The character with the highest net Attack bonus (excluding any inside her cauldron) must succeed a L5 magic save or be transformed into a giant frog-thing who attacks the party like a monster with a Level equal to the character's L+3. All equipment and weapons are thrown aside (no action needed) except underpants, which become violet. A Blessing spell or the

34

hag's death restores the character's original form. The equipment thrown aside remains in the cauldron and can only be retrieved after the hag is killed or flees. Any books or scrolls in the cauldron will be destroyed on a d6 roll of 1-3.

3-4 Drain*: The hag drains a Blessing spell from a random character who has that spell unspent (including scrolls or magic items). If none have it, she drains a Healing spell instead. If there is none either, she drains a random unspent spell, scroll or magic item of all charges.

5 Curse of Coldness: A random character becomes aloof and passionless, causing a -1 penalty to Attack rolls and to fail all persuasion and breeding saves. If you have TCOTFD, the character cannot woo anymore; any satyrs and succubi so afflicted lose d3 life from utter despair. Only a Blessing spell or potion can cure this. Married characters, if this condition is not cured, face a 1-2 in 6 chance of divorce after each further adventure.

6 Healing: The hag heals herself back to her original life points. Any negative magic effect she was under is canceled. Each time this spell is cast, the effort cumulatively reduces the hag's L by 2 (e.g. from

L9 to 7, then to 5, etc.). If she is under L3, the healing spell fails.

Add 1 soul cube to the hag's treasure each time she casts this spell.

Note 3 (Djinn): A subdued djinn will grant the party a single lesser wish in exchange for his/her freedom. A wish can be used to gain a single use Luck point (that works like the halfling ability of the same name), create any non-magical treasure or single piece of equipment worth 100 gp or less, a spell scroll of your choice (from any 4AD book you own, excluding spells of Expert or higher level) or a single permanent effect that gives a character a +1 bonus to a specific save (e.g. bigger muscles or bosom for a +1 to Persuasion saves).

Note 4 (Cheerful Cleric): If you have TTT, roll on the Gods of Norindaal table and mark 1 Friendly tick with one of the deity's alignments. Clerics of the gods of Life never condemn lovemaking, Blessing the party instead.

Note 5 (Desperate Dwarf): Drunk as a boar, Harros Davanzu is a dissolute young nobleman from Kardalok who lost his three rings of office (again). Treat this as the "Bring me that!" quest: each rings is at each at a separate place. A single reward of 300 gp is offered for finding all three rings. Alternately, if you have *Three Rings*, you can start that adventure even if you already completed it (the lad keeps losing the damned rings). Each goblin, harlequin or cleric of Gobras receives a Blessing upon encountering Davanzu (who may or not be the god's avatar) the first time.

Note 6 (Pegasi): Winged horses are rare and meeting them is a unique occurrence. If you roll this result again, your party encounters a small hamlet instead (one tile in size). You can sell equipment, gems, jewels, scrolls and magical treasures here and buy any item available from the 4AD book. Your party can also rest at the inn (for 1 gp and 1 life healed per character, per day). If your group is escorting any prisoners, this is their home. On a d6 roll of 5-6, the hamlet also has a small temple where you can buy healing potions, holy water, blessing scrolls and resurrection services for the usual price. Roll d6 for the town's dominant ethnicity: 1-4 humans, 5 halflings, 6 elves. Alternately, if you have TTT, you can generate a random small town 1 tile in size. In that case, ignore the rules for factions, Turmoil and Undercity.

Note 7 (Girdle of Sex Change): For most classes, sex change has no tangible game effect (except higher wardrobe expenses). Satyrs who put on the girdle change their class to become elves temporarily (their spells remain the same). Moonbeasts decrease in size and lose both 1 life per level and their size-based penalties. Ice elves, likewise, temporarily take the other sex's class. The girdle has no effect on succubi, golems and clerics of Gobras, who cannot wear it.

Note 8 (Evil Squirrels): These frightful rodents are considered rattish monsters for all purposes and can be bribed with 3 food . For every 13 of them killed (round down), any witchhunters in the party get a +1 bonus to Attack rolls and saves versus dark hags and their mistress Sister Eliza. That bonus cannot go above their current level.

Note 9 (Owlfolk Riding Dogs): Treat this encounter as peaceful. The owlfolk sell any non-magic, non-living items worth under 101 gp available in any 4AD book you own. In addition, they will also have any single magic potion worth 100 gp or less for sale on a d6 roll of 5-6, but never more than a total of d3 potions at any given time. If you encounter owlfolk again, it will be the same group on a d6 roll of 4-6 (always a "merchant" reaction) and its potion inventory will be replenished.

The Wicked Witch of the North-West, a dark hag, jealously guards the unlucky halfling she's invited over for lunch.